S⅂

MW01504352

HEART

and

SPIRIT

of a

MOTHER

God Bless
You Cassie!

Proverbs 3: 5-6

L. K. Alexander-Belford

12/17

STRAIGHT
from the
HEART
and
SPIRIT
of a
MOTHER

A MOTHER'S LOVE
LANGUAGE OF WISDOM AND
PRACTICAL ADVICE TO DAUGHTERS

L. K. ALEXANDER-BEDFORD

TATE PUBLISHING
AND ENTERPRISES, LLC

Published by Tate Publishing & Enterprises, LLC
127 E. Trade Center Terrace | Mustang, Oklahoma 73064 USA
1.888.361.9473 | www.tatepublishing.com

Tate Publishing is committed to excellence in the publishing industry. The company reflects the philosophy established by the founders, based on Psalm 68:11,
"The Lord gave the word and great was the company of those who published it."

Book design copyright © 2014 by Tate Publishing, LLC. All rights reserved.
Cover design by Rtor Maghuyop
Interior design by Gram Telen

Published in the United States of America

ISBN: 978-1-63268-592-6
1. Religion / Christian Life / General
2. Religion / Christian Life / Inspirational
15.05.13

How much better to get wisdom than gold, and to choose understanding rather than silver!

Proverbs 16:16

To
My Beloved Daughters
Lisa Dawn Davis and Alexis Lynne Davis Smith
My Good Treasure, My Best Investment,
and Celebration of My Life!

Contents

Part II
Girl Talk

Part III
Friendship

Part IV
As The World Turns

Part V
Marriage

Part VI
Motherhood & Children

Foreword

Since I was a little girl, several of my friends wished they had the kind mother I have – one you can confide in, laugh with, share even your most intimate thoughts, and the kind of mother who is also a best friend.

To this day, my girlfriends are amazed at the special relationship that my sister Lisa and I share with our mom – and the fact that I talk with her every day about everything: life, career, family, friendship, male-female relationships or marriage and, most especially, God. "You told your mom what? I could never say that to my mom," or "What did your mom say?" are some of the questions and responses I often receive.

The truth is, I am often amazed that they, and many women out there, don't have close and friendly relationships with their moms. How could that be, I wonder? However, over the years, I have discovered that my mom is and always has been different from other mothers, not better and not necessarily more loving, just much cooler. She is special!

My mom has consistently been the woman I most admire, respect, and revere. She has been my shelter, my protector, my cheerleader, my guide, my counselor, and my coach. Over the years, she has imparted great advice to me, sometimes little nuggets and other times, long "on-the-couch" sessions. Each time, they have been words of wisdom laced by the right combination of spirituality, real-world experience, personal insight, respect, and encouragement, embraced by a lot of love without judgment. I might be biased, but I have always believed that my mom is the most awesome woman in the world. She's beautiful, smart, funny, sincere, and most of all, a good listener.

When you are a little girl, you think your parents know everything. Well, I'm in my early forties and still think that. And I am not alone. People have always been drawn to my mom like a magnet. They want to talk with her, share with her, many walk away wishing they had just a piece of what she has – not in terms of material things or looks – but in the power she possesses in being her own woman, a strong woman, confident in her strength and living totally by her faith in God through Jesus Christ.

My sister Lisa and I, among many other young women who unofficially adopted our mom as their own, have been blessed by her for many years, either because of her actions, words, honesty, or her sheer presence.

Through this amazing book, my sister and I are proud to share a little piece of our mom with you. I, personally hope *Straight from the Heart & Spirit of a Mother* blesses and assists you in finding the right direction for many of life's curves as it has for us. For those of you who don't have a mother, or not in a positive mother-daughter relationship, or just need some supplemental advice from an experienced, spiritually-grounded, and sincere resource, this book is for you!

ALEXIS DAVIS SMITH
Proud to say, the daughter and best friend of L.K. Alexander-Bedford

Introduction

For in Him., we live, and move and have our being;…

Acts 17:28

I love to give God praise and thanksgiving… especially for my precious jewels and good treasure—my daughters Lisa Dawn and Alexis Lynne. Their love, respect, and faith in me was affirmation to begin the journey to write *Straight from the Heart and Spirit of a Mother.*

It was Alexis, my younger, who said to me, almost a decade ago, "Mom, you should write a book. You have always given Lisa and me great advice. I think of your advice as golden nuggets of wisdom." She added, "You've not only helped Lisa and me, you've helped some of our friends too. I think that other women, young and old, could benefit from some of the words of wisdom like we have."

Later, I thought about what Alexis said, however, I must admit I was a little hesitant at first. Shortly after that conversation, I called Lisa, my older daughter, and asked her to share with me some of my advice that benefited her most. I was surprised by her responses and had forgotten until she quoted me verbatim words I had spoken to her.

Not long after I gave serious thought about what the girls shared with me during those conversations. I felt very encouraged that I really had something worthwhile to say to other women as well as my daughters. Within a few days, I picked up a pen and yellow legal pad and began the writing process. I was surprised how thoughts just poured out and gave me a feeling of confirmation that I needed to do this.

Straight from the Heart… is a compilation for what I believe is practical and sound advice, written with a purpose to either inspire, encourage, empower, spiritually elevate, or simply enlighten you the reader, especially in this postmodern era.

My writings come straight from the heart and spirit based on my personal experiences, observations, and learning from trials and errors. Before I began to write, I knew I had to seek God's direction first—so I prayed for His anointing and wisdom. As a result, without sounding preachy, each piece has been written with God, my Father and Jesus Christ, my Savior in mind; and supported by *The Holy Scriptures* from both the *King James Version* and the *New International Version* (NIV).

I believe these "nuggets" of personal thoughts and advice, in some way, will benefit you as they have my daughters. It is also my hope and purpose that you'll share a page or so with other women; and perhaps, men too!

Finally, *Straight from the Heart...* even though it was written specifically for Lisa and Alexis, I humbly dedicate this publication to daughters everywhere – regardless of age, crossing racial lines, and religious barriers. My desire is that this book will bless your heart and spirit and benefit you in some special way. In addition, that you'll want to share it with others.

—L. K. Alexander-Bedford

In Memory of those persons who touched or changed my life in a special way.

Lucretia Webb Alexander, my mother, who instilled strong moral and spiritual values in my three siblings and me early.

The Rev. James Lloyd Webb, my "Pop Pop," who profoundly impacted my spiritual journey by his Christian example as well as inheriting his gift of written and verbal communication. His favorite hymn, "On Christ the Solid Rock I Stand," continues to resonate in my spirit today.

Katie Lee Alexander, my paternal grandmother, fondly called "Nana." I believe I inherited her strength, assertiveness, serving others, and great love for family and friends.

Ethel Bell Webb, my beloved aunt. When she said, "I love you," I could always feel it!

Rose Galloway, I call my "Titus Woman." She touched my life in an incredible way, from childhood to becoming a young adult. She was a God-send and a very special blessing who encouraged me "to fly."

Charles H. Peoples, my fifth grade teacher, William Dick Elementary School, Philadelphia, PA. When I think of having a positive self-esteem, it was his confidence in me that helped me to believe in myself having been a shy little girl.

C. Delores Tucker, powerful and renowned – yet a humble role model who possessed a beautiful Christian spirit. She left a lasting impression on me the very first time I met her while I was Youth Editor at *The Philadelphia Tribune*. I said to myself, "I want to be like her."

and

Alexis Lynn Alexander, my younger sister, whom the Lord called home to Glory at a very early age. I carry "Lynn Lynn" in my heart and named my second daughter Alexis after her.

This Life Is a Faith Journey
Not Meant to Be Easy
It's a Maturation Process

Walking with God daily is a faith journey.
We learn and grow through trials and errors along the way.

The key to staying on the path is
letting nothing distract you from your faith
and trust in God through Jesus Christ.

Keep your focus by trying to keep His Commandments;
believing and trusting in Him; and
reading and studying His Word.

It's not always easy.
Pray to the Lord to help you when times are difficult.
He will honor your requests in His way and time
because He is faithful to those who believe.
He will be your refuge and strength

through all your struggles and life's storms
when you truly depend on Him.
God alone controls the whole world.
He also promises to give you
the desires of your heart and rewards too.
It's all about faith!
To have faith, you **must believe**!

And without faith it is impossible to please God, because anyone who comes to Him must believe that He exists and that He rewards those who earnestly seek Him.

Hebrews 11:6

Everyone Has Value
and So Do You!

God created us all!
No person is better than another
regardless of family origin, color,
background, or living environment.

Pass on to your children, grandchildren, nieces,
and nephews… that everyone has value
as such, always show them respect.

Try to see others through God's eyes.
Don't judge or measure them by today's
so-called standards or values:
titles, popularity, celebrity, or financial status.
Today, it's so easy to follow the crowd
and become sidetracked if
you don't think for yourself.
Beat your own drum!

Don't allow your peers to set your
standards by following them.

Be confident and set your own standards.
Be mindful of worldly things and the messages they send.
Remember, you are in the world, but not of the world.
You please God when you show love,
compassion, and respect for others.

....

*Not that we are competent in ourselves to claim
anything for ourselves, but our competence comes from
God.*

II Corinthians 3:5

A Daily Dose Strongly Recommended by Mom

KEEP GOD FIRST!

Count each day a blessing because it's made by God.
Make it a habit to thank Him before you begin your day.
Commit to having daily prayer (talk
to Him) and read His Word
whether it's the Bible or a biblical devotional.

This will jump-start your day, renew your mind,
and lift your spirit.

Keep the Lord first
even if it takes getting out of bed a little earlier.
It will make a positive difference in your life
and bless you.

Keep God first no matter what!

L. K. Alexander-Bedford

But first seek His kingdom and His righteousness, and all these things will be given to you...

Matthew 6:33

Winners in God's Eyes

You are royalty!
You are a winner in God's eyes.
After all, He made you…
Everything He makes is beyond good!

There's no such thing as luck, fate,
or chance regarding the children of God.

In the world, only persons of elite status are those who
walk with Presidents, Premiers, kings, and queens,
however, in God's eyes, we are His elect.

We are all the same because He
chose us to walk with Him.
He's Supreme and we are royalty.

---

*…because the One who is in you is greater than the one
in the world.*

I John 4:4

Take Pleasure in Being You!
You are Somebody!

Don't compare yourself or try to compete
with your peers or others.
You are you, unique, one of a kind
and preciously made by God.
He has a purpose for your life.
Once you discover it, appreciate it, and celebrate you,
but do it in humbleness.

Always be true to yourself.
Live your life for you, but unto God first!
Others will treat and respect you the way you
treat yourself.

No, not everyone is going to like you.
That's reality!
But they will respect you if you demand it!

It's okay to speak freely your thoughts and verbalize

what you feel and want, whether it
is with a woman or man.

Always be you!
Don't allow others to define who you are.
That's your God-given prerogative and power
based on standards you set for yourself.

Represent!
Have confidence. Always speak up for yourself.
Accept no intimidation from anyone.

Stand up!
Be your own woman.
Feel good about being you and loving you
as long as it's without vanity.

LOVE!
It's easy to love others when you love yourself!

I praise You because I am fearfully and wonderfully made.

Psalm 139:14

Filled with His Right Stuff

We live in a society where everybody loves a winner.
Where "thin is in" and good looks open doors.
Having a prestigious title before your name
says you are somebody.
Driving a luxury car and living in
an upscale neighborhood
means you have arrived.

Some people think or use these things
to validate themselves and/or seek acceptance
as well or praise from others.

Be very careful not to let the culture define
or validate who you are.
Stay true to yourself without the labels.

You love you!
Respect yourself as you respect others.

Know this, there's only one true validation that matters.
That's God!
He should matter most because He's the one Who made
and put His divine stamp on you.
If you don't believe that, you'll never be satisfied.

---

*Delight yourself in the Lord and He will give you the
desires of your heart.*

Psalms 37:4

It Makes Perfect Sense
to Please God Rather Than Man

If you don't want your life to go around in a circle,
try pleasing God rather than man.
It's really not difficult.

Don't allow anyone to make you feel less
than how God made and sees you…
Beautiful!

He's the One Who has a divine plan
for your life if you only trust Him.

All power is in His hands.

Don't allow anyone to stifle or rob you of that power.

*For God did not give us a spirit of timidity,
but a spirit of power, love and self-discipline.*

II Timothy 1:7

The Choices We Make
Some Good – Some Bad
Be Careful!

We all make bad choices even if it's not intentional.
That's part of the human condition.

We moms are not exempt.
I certainly made mine, but I learned from them
so I wouldn't make them a second or third time.

May your bad choices be few and in between.
Most of all, I hope you learn from them and allow
them to become life lessons.

I pray that you become wiser as a result;
that your faith will be stretched and increased;
and the end result will be to call on God.

Trust Him with the choices you make as you wait patiently, listen and try to please Him. Don't allow your emotions to run away with you.

....

I will instruct you and teach you in the way you should go; I will counsel you and watch over you.

Psalm 32:8

Consider the Consequences
Before Acting on Quick Decisions

Try never to make a decision when you are emotional,
stressed, or under pressure.

Always wait!
Always pray!
It pays to sleep on it too!

Wait for the calm.
What a difference it will make.

Self-centered decisions can often result
in disastrous consequences
that could have been prevented.

God ALWAYS knows what you are going through.
Be wise!
Seek Him first and trust Him
to help you make decisions that you won't regret.

May God perfect, establish, strengthen and settle you.

I Peter 5:10

Cancel Out Fear with Faith

You have the Power
to realize Your dreams and goals.

Don't allow fear to hold you back.

Walk in faith!
Your keyword is F-A-I-T-H
because faith cancels out fear.

Trust yourself to take risks…
If not, you could miss out on something good,
something God has just for you!
Don't miss your blessing!

---

*In all your ways acknowledge Him,
and He will make your paths straight.*

Proverbs 3:6

Troubled and Don't Know What to Do?

There will be times you have problems
but have no idea how to solve them.
You'll feel led to do something,
but you just don't know what.
What do you do?

The answer is simple, but very true.
Do nothing! Absolutely nothing!

Don't go ahead of God!
Seek Him for His guidance…

First pray and then wait!
Be patient!

When you seek Him first, He will be
faithful to either take you through it,
around it, or over it.

Remember Who is in control.
Again, wait!

God knows what is best
and always has His best for you!

He'll bring you out His way.
Nothing else will compare.

Wait for the Lord; be strong and take heart…He is our help and our shield.

Psalms 27:14 & 33:30

"Let Go and Let God"
Is More Than an Expression

When you feel the need to let go and let God,
Do it! Give your problem to Him.

Sometimes, it's not easy to give it to Him initially.
You might have to go through the process more than once
before letting it go.
That's okay! God understands.

When you do let it go, you'll know because
you no longer worry, no longer stress,
or take it to your pillow.

You'll know you have released it because
you will experience peace–God's peace.

···

And the peace of God, which transcends all understanding will guard your hearts and minds in Christ Jesus.

Philippians 4:7

Commitments and Promises Are Matters of Priorities

People always do what their priorities are.

Don't fret or get bent out of shape when loved ones
or friends sometimes disappoint you by not keeping
their word whether it's a commitment or promise to you.

What's a priority to you might not be a priority to them.
When they disappoint you, it's clear
that you are not a priority.

If you were, that promise or commitment would be kept
unless a situation came up that they had no control over.

So don't pout. Don't get mad.
Learn from this:
whatever the priority is what people do.

Always stay committed to your priorities.

....

...Honor one another above yourselves.

Romans 12:10

It's Not Vanity in Loving Self

It's okay to love yourself without being vain.
Loving self encompasses self-confidence, self-respect,
and most of all, respect for others.

When you learn how to love you,
it's easy to love others.

The greatest love of all is your love for God,
then others as well as yourself.

Everyone needs love…

Share the love!

Faith works through love.

Galatians 5:6

Attitude Matters

Regardless of your circumstances, especially
if they are undeserving or simply bad,
you have the power within to handle them
for the better.

It depends on your attitude, bad or positive.
It's a matter of choice.
You can choose to be bitter, angry, or unforgiving.
The better choice is to focus on the positive.

Use the power within you.
Don't allow a negative attitude to rob your
joy, peace or freedom.

Hanging on to a negative attitude is a lose-lose situation.
Who cares?
A positive attitude is always a win-win situation
and it feels good!

....

Finally, brothers [sisters]. Whatever is true, whatever is right, whatever is pure, whatever is lovely… think on such things.

Philippians 4:8

Judge Not Right or Wrong
Look for the Best in Others

People are different…

Initially, what you look for in others is what you will
be drawn to or what you think you see,
but not necessarily what you'll find.

You will not become disappointed if you
try to look beyond the surface and look for their good,
true, and sincere qualities.

You will be disappointed if you measure
others by your standards other than who they
really are – the positive and the negative.
We all have some of both.
But it's what we choose that makes the difference.

None of us have lived our lives so perfectly
that we can judge others.

No matter what, we should show love.

Remember, God is the only one to judge.

DO NOT judge or you too will be judged.

Matthew 7:1

Plan Ahead for the Ones You Love and Respect

Make those you love a priority when it comes
to showing love and appreciation.
You know in advance his/her special day is coming.

Birthday, Anniversary, Mother's/Father's Day…
or any significant occasion.
Don't wait until the last minute
to express your love and to show you care by sending a
card, gift, or making a phone call.
Do not text your greeting to those you love and care about,
especially your parents, grandparents, or aunts and uncles.

Plan ahead and make their day!

*May the Lord repay you for what you have done. May
you be richly rewarded by the Lord.*

Ruth 2:12

Be Grateful!
It Goes a Long Way

Do not let today's trends and culture set your standards
in terms of expressing gratitude when
someone does something
nice for you, especially when she/
he goes out of her/his way.
Keep in mind, she/he didn't have to do anything.

Take out the time to acknowledge your gratitude.
Write a note of thanks or at least call.
Your benefactor deserves more than a text or e-mail
even if YOU think it's politically correct.

MOMS, teach that to your children too!

*...in everything give thanks, for this is the will of God
in Jesus Christ for you.*

I Thessalonians 5:18

We Are Family!

Regardless of our beliefs and differences;
negative situations; and relatives who get a charge out of
chaos, confusion, confrontation, or drama,
show love at all times and remain loyal.

Family is family, something we don't choose, but we are
to love them anyway, even when we disagree.

Keep family business within the family even if you
don't care for his/her ways or dislike
the person, don't make
his or her problem your problem, don't
stop loving the individual.
Love them in the Spirit of the Lord.

Learn to forgive as Christ forgave us on the cross
and time after time–and pray for the individual.

You might can't change the circumstance or situation,

but only YOU can change how you deal with either.

One thing that is certain:
We are family no matter what!

....

*Finally, all of you be of one mind, having compassion
for one another, love as brother [sister]…*

I Peter 3:8

Treasure Your Elders
and Show Love!

Treasure your parents, grandparents, aunts, and uncles…
especially as they grow older.
Be mindful about showing them how
much you love and care about them.

Take a minute or time out of your schedule and bless them
with a phone call (not a text or e-mail,)
visit, or send a notecard…
Don't stop there, remember their
birthdays and special occasions
with a card, flowers, or even a fitting gift.

Pass this on to your children.
Keep in mind:

Someday, if you live long enough, you'll
become somebody's elder…
and prayerfully, receive the same loving blessings.

....

The glory of young men [women] is their strength; and the beauty of old men [women] is their gray hair...

Proverbs 20:29

Let Your Light Shine for God

Today's world greatly needs women who will
stand boldly for God and Jesus Christ.

Women who are committed to live out their faith,
not simply in conversation, but in action with boldness
and humbleness.

Let your Light shine!

Talk it…

Walk it…

Share it!

Most of all, live it!

You are the salt of the earth... You are the light of the world...

Matthew 5:13-14

Whether You Believe or Not God Is Your EVERY Answer and More!

I am not telling you this because I heard a Bible scholar
or a pastor say it, or because I read The Holy Bible.

I say, God is every answer because it's the gospel truth
and to know is to believe!

I know what I am talking about
because I've experienced Him
for myself and His faithfulness.

When you come to trust and know Him like that,
You, too, will say, "He is and He's real."

You'll know He is your only Answer too!

....

Every word of God is flawless:
He is a shield to those who take refuge in Him.

Proverbs 30:5

It's All in God's *Word*

My advice to all women is not to be satisfied with simply
knowing about or believing there is a God.

If you seriously desire to know Him personally,
I encourage you to pursue Him and
get to know Him intimately.

Find a Bible-teaching church and take your Bible.
Attend worship service and Bible study regularly.
Make them priorities.

Don't wait for Sunday to come—get to know God
by communicating with Him in prayer, the first thing
in the morning and last thing at night.
You can even talk to him lying on your pillow.

Get in the habit of spending quality time with Him.
Read and study the Holy Bible.
Everything you need to know is there in The Book.

L. K. Alexander-Bedford

....

Thy Word is a lamp unto my feet, and a light unto my faith.

Psalm 119:105

A Childlike Faith
Is Faith with Purpose

To have faith, one must believe in God.
It's easier said than demonstrated.

Having faith is a challenge, especially for new believers.
It can be an ongoing challenge…
It's a matter of exercising a Childlike faith – similar to
the faith we had in our parents as a child.
By exercising that Childlike faith,
one grows into becoming
God's true believer.

Do you recall as a child when Mom told you, "Take your
umbrella with you because it's going
to rain?" But you thought
to yourself, "It's not going to rain," but
you took your umbrella anyway.

Lo and behold, it rained.
That's what's called Childlike faith and the kind of faith
God expects from us.

We believe Him just because He says so!

---

*Now faith is the substance of things hoped for,
the evidence of things not seen.*

Hebrews 11:1

You Don't Have to
Be Anxious for Anything…
Really!

When you believe in your heart and sincerely turn your
earthly worries over to God,
He will answer your prayer and give
you His Heavenly peace.

Turn to Philippians 4:6

"Do not be anxious about anything, but
in every thing by prayer and petition, with
thanksgiving, present your requests to God."

GOD IS YOUR
POWER and SOURCE

Allow God, and He alone, to become
the power source to meet
your needs and desires.

He owns and controls EVERYTHING!
No matter what we humans think or say, God is all Power!

God is the ONLY source and power of everything
and for EVERYTHING you need!

For the kingdom of God is not a matter of talk but of power.

I Corinthians 4:20

Just the Right Tools to Use
for Unkind Situations

God offers you the perfect tools to
handle any stressful or hurtful
situation.
Those tools are at your disposal – right there in *The Book.*
All you have to do is search the Scriptures.

If you don't know where to begin,
start in the book of Proverbs
and also search the Psalms.
You can also seek guidance from a pastor or minister.

God is almighty and faithful!
He's the only One who never lies or lets you down.
Even when you are faithless, He remains faithful!

You can stand on God's Holy Word
and His numerous promises.

Believe in Him and believe His Word and promises. Your resolve will come from your perseverance and standing the test by trusting Him.

....

Trust in the LORD *with all your heart and lean not on your own understanding; in all your ways acknowledge Him, and He will make your paths straight.*

Proverbs 3:5

The Opposite of Fear
Is Your Unused Faith

When troubles come and they will.
That's the time to exercise your faith in God,
even if it's the size of a "grain of a mustard seed,"
according to Matthew 17:20.

You CAN trust God
no matter how things feel or look.

God is right there waiting to take the weight off you
if you'll only turn to Him in prayer.

He loves and cares for you no matter
what, even if your problem
is as small as a bee sting or prick in your finger.

A hymn writer penned it best:

"O what peace we often forfeit,

L. K. Alexander-Bedford

O what needless pains we bear, all because
We do not carry everything to God in prayer."

The Lord is my Helper; I will not be afraid. What can man do to me?

Hebrews 13:6

There Are No Quick Fixes

Today, we live in a hurry-hurry and worry-worry world.
When trials come, we want a quick fix, even from God.
We want Him to instantly make our
troubles disappear, so we can
feel good again and go back to things as usual.

God will always intervene and help us when
we are patient and wait on Him.
His desire is for us to give Him total surrender;
be patient, trust and wait on Him.
Yes, WAIT!

Because we want that quick fix,
sometimes we become impatient
and sabotage His answer. Or when
He answers, we return to the
same old behavior — hurry-hurry and worry-worry.

If we trust Him and simply wait, victory will come.
He'll answer again if we CONTINUE
to trust Him and wait…

The LORD *delights in those who fear Him, who put
their hope in His unfailing love.*

Psalm 147:11

Sometimes God Uses Our Circumstances for His Purpose

Have you ever prayed and prayed, read your Bible,
and asked others to pray for you too, but nothing changed.
While waiting, did you wonder why God
was taking so long to answer?

When the change took place, what
was the lesson you learned?
Could it be that God was teaching and transforming you?

Think about it, when God desires to
transform or refine us for the better,
He stretches and tests us. Sometimes, by
disciplining us, ultimately using
our circumstances to draw us closer
to Him and grow our faith
so we can be more fruitful for Him.

Whatever the circumstance is, His
purpose results in blessings
if we believe, listen—and with a sincere
heart, truly trust Him.

Note: The Old Testament suggests God
sometimes inflicts suffering, however, it was
the blood of Jesus that we overcome.

---

*But the God of all grace, who called us unto His eternal
glory by Christ Jesus, after that ye have suffered a while,
make you perfect, establish, strengthen, and settle you.*

I Peter 5:10

What's Your Pain/Pleasure?
You Can Back Up or Drown

Whenever you feel you are walking
in deep water and think
you are going to drown because of a bad decision,
immediately back up!

That decision does not have to result in a negative
or catastrophic consequence.

You don't have to drown.

Simply begin to back up and then turn around.

Then stop!

Look up!

L. K. Alexander-Bedford

Look to the Light – Look up to God!

He always gives us a way out.

I will lift up my eyes unto the hills–from whence cometh my help.

Psalm 121:1

God Always Answers Prayer – But His Way!

You might not agree to His answer, but
God always answers prayer.

Sometimes, His answer is yes.
Sometimes, His answer is wait.
Sometimes, His answer is better than you could imagine.

Don't think because you read your
Bible or pray daily that God is
going to always answer your desires or requests.

Ask yourself, "Am I living my life according to His will?"
"Am I giving Him my time and first fruits?"
"Do I have the right to ask for anything
in the name of Jesus?"

If the answer is no, what are you going to do about it?

....

The prayer of the righteous man is powerful and effective.

James 5:16

Your Most Prized Gift Can't be Found Inside a Store

Your greatest most prized gift comes from God
in the form of His Son Jesus Christ.
Your greatest gift back to Him is trying to
please Him by loving Him with your all
Loving Him with your all and all, loving one another
and trying to live your life pleasing and holy unto Him.

Love the LORD *with all your heart and with all your soul and with all your strength.*

Deuteronomy 6:5

There Are No Quick Fixes

When trials come, we want a quick fix from God.

We want Him to instantly make our problems disappear
so we can be happy again and go
back to business as normal.

God hears our prayers and will always answer us.
More than that, His desire is for us
to give Him total surrender
to make us not only content, but to make us whole.
In some situations, there's a lesson He wants us to learn.

If we only trust Him and wait…
His victory is sure to come!

The LORD *delights in those who fear Him, who put
their hope in His unfailing love.*

Psalm 147:11

The Best Things in Life Are Definitely Not the Bling-Bling…

Things that make a significant difference in life are FREE
and too often are overlooked or taken for granted.

They are things we all need but cannot be bought or sold
because they are priceless!

They begin with:
The love of God, His first gift
His Son Jesus Christ, God with us–along
with the Holy Spirit, our Comforter.

Nothing compares because they are
valuables that have no price tags.
They are the very best things in life,
worth more than silver and gold.

···

Every good and perfect gift is from above...

James 1:7

Desire Real Success?
Commit to God and Use
Your Gift(s) to His Glory!

God gives everyone a special gift.

Some people are blessed with more than one, but all are specific for the individual.

Once you discover yours, the best way you can show God gratitude is by crafting and using your gift to glorify Him.

In return, you are sure to win divine success. The success that lasts.

Commit to the Lord whatever you do, and your plans will succeed.

Proverbs 16:3

Stuff Is Only Stuff
It Will Never Satisfy

Stay in touch with the realities of life instead
of the popularity of Reality-TV
Don't allow today's culture and trends
drive or/and define who you are.

It's so easy to let stuff–what's popular
or your possessions possess you.

The things of this world never last!

Today, too many women, young and old, are caught up
with their stuff.

Some can never attain enough, the more
they get, the more stuff they want.

Money buys things.
Yes, THINGS!

However, it can't buy real life and real living such as:
LOVE, PEACE of mind, JOY,
HAPPINESS or Contentment.

There's nothing wrong with possessing nice stuff
as long as that nice stuff doesn't possess you!

Watch out! Be on guard against all kinds of greed....For
where your treasure is there will your heart be also.

Luke 12:15, 34

Who Completes You?
God Can!

Many women in today's world fell prey to the movie line,
"You complete me," from the 1999 Jerry McGuire flick.
Not thinking for themselves, they believe
that it takes a man to complete them.

The truth is, until we women learn that
only God can complete us, we'll
never feel whole – woman or man.

Genuine and lasting satisfaction come
from Above – the God in us.
It's our relationship with Him that we truly
will know love; how to love, give love,
and receive love.

Without thinking, we embrace
society's vision of wholeness.

Until we understand our need for a relationship
with God, there will always be
a vacuum inside that needs filling.

True fulfillment begins and ends with a
relationship that keeps God first and center.
Trust Him and the rest will come together.

For in Him we live, move and have our being.

Acts 17:28

Defeating the Schemer's Temptations Listen to Your Inner Voice

From time to time, when things are going well, some
form of temptation will knock at your door. If you
are unaware what's going on, the schemer, the Devil
will play tricks with your mind and take it to a place
you hadn't planned to go or even stay for a while.

The Holy Spirit will help you by telling
you, "You don't want to do that."
But the mind is weak and will tell you,
"It's okay – who's going to know?"
You are left with the decision to make a choice–to adhere
to the Holy Spirit, Who protects you over your flesh
or succumb to the Devil whose aim is to destroy and
will even try to kill…

L. K. Alexander-Bedford

Either you'll obey the Holy Spirit's
leading or be led by the clever one.
The choice is yours to either serve God or the Devil.
If you choose to listen to your inner voice, the
Holy Spirit, He will always give you a way out
of the situation – simply CALL ON GOD!
He will not forsake you!

We, the Believers, hear three voices who speak – the
Holy Spirit's – our inner voice and the enemy's.
The question is to whom will you listen?

You must guard your mind by being mindful
of the enemy's various tricks and devices.
It's amazing how many people believe
there's a real God but not a real Devil.

*God is faithful, He will not let you be tempted beyond
what you can bear...He will provide a way out so that
you can stand under it.*

I Corinthians 10:13

Our Parents and Our Forgiveness

Our Holy Bible tells us to honor our parents…

Depending on the circumstance that
can be difficult and a huge
challenge for some,
especially daughters who have not had a loving or
close relationship with their moms.

No matter what, we must forgive
because Jesus Christ said so.

If we don't forgive them for their
offenses, no matter how deep
our hurt or pain, we tie ourselves up in knots
and voluntarily imprison ourselves
and not recognize it.

If we are obedient to God's Word and
forgive them with sincerity,

the healing process will begin and free us.

Most importantly, we honor our
Father. He in turn will honor
our forgiveness and set us free.

When we do, we imitate Our Savior Jesus
Christ, the One who forgives
and Who has pinned our sins of forgiveness to the cross.

Honor your father and mother, which is the first commandment with a promise; that it may go well with you and that you may enjoy long life on earth.

Ephesians 6:2-3

Don't Allow Unforgiving to Imprison You—Because It Can!

If you live long enough, there will
come a time when somebody
you love or respect will deeply disappoint
or betray you and/or cause pain.
The pain cuts so deeply, you feel you'll never get over it.
But you can!

Nothing compares to a test of one's
faith like unforgiveness.
It can consume you, keep you angry, make you unhappy,
and weigh you down with resentment.

Regardless of how strong your spiritual beliefs,
you can find it difficult to forgive.
But you must!
Why, God says so! It's His mandate.

If you choose not to forgive your betrayer,
you hold yourself in hostage.
You imprison yourself and the adversary could care less.

Forgiveness frees and draws you closer to God, Who
in turn will handle your enemy because of your obedience.

Your blessing is freedom with God's peace,
the peace that passes all understanding.

Keep in mind, once you forgive, it doesn't
mean you're obligated to bring
that person up close and personal again.

You can continue to love her/him, but you
might have to keep her/him at a distance.

How great is God's forgiveness!

Forgive as the Lord forgave you.

Colossians 3:13

Part II

Girl Talk

About Men and Relationships

See Yourself as a Treasure
Not Some Man's Trophy

Beloved daughters, you are God's precious treasure,
not some guy's trophy.

You must see yourself from God's viewpoint.
Don't allow anyone to make you feel
less than the beautiful creation
God made you to be.

You have been wonderfully and fearfully made.
You don't have to settle…

…for I am fearfully and wonderfully made, marvelous
are Your works.

Psalm 139:14

If You're Looking for Love Begin by Loving Yourself

Just because your Mr. Right has not
surfaced, don't be dismayed.

Don't get caught up thinking or believing that it takes
a man to make you happy or complete you.

Remember: You are a child of God.

Work on you! Learn how to be content
and love yourself without vanity.
If that's difficult, what do you expect
to bring to a relationship?

A man cannot fulfill you, but he can
enhance and elevate what you feel
and believe and respect about yourself.

You have the control to feel whole by letting
God complete you rather than man.

Put God first! Pray to Him and ask to
align you with just the right guy.
Trust Him. Be patient and He will.

---

*Delight yourself in the Lord and He will give you the
desires of your heart.*

Psalm 37:4

Ladies: You Don't Have to Settle EVER!

Don't ever think you have to settle for a man regardless
of your age or you think there is a shortage of men.
Who knows?

Don't settle for less than what you deserve.
He should be the so-called "Mr. Perfect,"
as long as he is the perfect man God has just for you.

Recognize what you want in a man.
Someone who will love, respect, adore you,
and accept you for whom you are.

Refuse to settle for one who is never
satisfied; who wants to make you over
or tries to control you. Pay attention to the signs.

A real man will love you for your
weaknesses as well as your strengths.

He's the type who simply loves you
for you and unconditionally.

You should desire a sure thing – not a good thing.
It's important that he connects with
your spiritual beliefs and family.
He should be one who can prove himself
trustworthy and loyal to you.

Have a checklist–for example:
Is he trustworthy?

Is he a person with whom you could
spend the rest of your life?
Would you be proud for him to be father of your children?

Can he protect and keep you safe?
Can he take care of you if you become ill and
can't contribute finance to the household?

Most importantly, are you both equally
yoked regarding your spiritual beliefs?

....

*Trust in the Lord with all your heart...In all your
ways acknowledge Him, and He will make your paths
straight.*

Proverbs 3:5-6

Don't Buy Into the Lies
You Hear Today

Ladies, beware!

Don't buy into the hype and lies of the
new woman syndrome, such as,
you can't be picky …

Set your standards on high and live by them.

Don't allow the world to define who you are.

Be mindful you are God's woman – one of
His best and measured by His standards,
like women described in Esther, Ephesians,
Proverbs, Titus, Hebrews, etc.

Be the best woman you can be, not for man, but for you.

God made you beautiful as well as wonderful and fearful.

He has instilled His power in you.
Be confident and walk in it!

....

Who can find a virtuous woman? For her price is far above rubies.

Proverbs 31:11

You Can Pick and Choose…

Beloved Daughters,

You don't have to settle for a husband or just any man.
Unfortunately, many women do.

Regardless of the trends of today;
what your peers choose to do;
or the fact that your clock is ticking
fast–you can pick and choose.

Don't become desperate by allowing your
emotions to rule over your heart.

Don't allow your peers or anyone drive you…

Pray to God that desire of your heart.

Trust and wait on Him to send you the man just for you.

It pays to wait and not regret!

Remember, you are in the world, but not of the world.

There's only one relationship that makes you truly whole.
And that's with Jesus!

However, it pleases Him for
you to pray for the desire of your heart—just the right man.

....

*Do not be anxious about anything, but in everything,
by prayer and petition, with thanksgiving, present your
requests to God.*

Philippians 4:6

God Shows Us Signs—Pay Attention!

If you find yourself in a relationship
and constantly going through
negative changes, some kind of drama or
conflict, you need to take a moment
to weigh the pros and cons about
your future with that person.

Pay attention to all the signs.

When your spirit mind/first mind warns
you to slow down and look
at the real picture, that might be a red flag.

If your gut/spirit-mind tells you to stop
– you need to end the relationship.
If you don't, you can risk hurt and pain
you will be destined to regret.

L. K. Alexander-Bedford

DO NOT!
Do not ignore the signs.

....

For God has not given us a spirit of timidity, but a spirit of power, of love and self-discipline.

II Timothy 1:7

Talking About the "P" Word...
Don't Compromise Your Power

Don't allow any guy's opinion determine your self-worth.
Be proud, but stay humble in terms of who you are.
Most of all, don't forget Whose you are and
Whose Power in which you walk.
Men will treat you the way you treat yourself.
Remember, we teach others how to treat us.
If you entertain opinions of others to
either accept or validate you,
you can easily surrender your power to them.
Think about it–that's too much power to give up!

....

God is my strength and power: And He makes my way perfect.

II Samuel 22:33

If You Can't Trust Him from the Beginning, You Have a Problem…

If you cannot trust your man from
the get-go because of one
discretion or more, don't rationalize or
think for one minute he'll change.
Don't fool yourself.
He won't!

If you allow your emotions to take over, you'll eventually
come to regret your decision. Don't let your heart
rule your mind and throw caution to the wind by
giving him a chance anyway. Most likely you'll regret it.

WARNING: Keep in mind, love
without trust will diminish.
It will hurt and keep hurting if YOU allow it.

One more thing:
If you choose to settle, **you'll be cheating** yourself.

What will that say about you?
Can you live with the answer?

Delight yourself in the LORD *and He will give you the desires of your heart.*

Psalm 37:4

Beware of How a Potential Mate Handles Conflict

Dealing with conflict with some men can be dangerous!
You must check out any man who
affectionately claims he sincerely
cares or is in love with you, especially if you
believe he's the one and considering marriage.

Check him out – things like:

His family background and their beliefs.
Does his belief align with yours?
Or does he believe at all?
How he was reared?
Who was his male role model?
Who taught him how to be a man?
Does he respect his mother?

How does he handle disagreements, especially anger?
Is he the controlling type?

Does he have double standards: one for
himself and another for you?
If he has a problem handling the other, most likely, he has
deeper problems, problems that won't change.

Most likely, his negative actions will escalate.

You need to think about these things.
They spell CAUTION!

You should desire someone with
whom you can build bridges
and not potential walls that imprison.

---

*Do not make friends with a hot-tempered man, do not
associate with one easily angered, or you may learn his
ways and get yourself ensnared.*

Proverbs 22:24-25

You Can't Push a Round Peg into a Square Hole No Matter How Hard You Try

You know when a relationship is not working.
So why push it?
Weigh the pros against the cons.
In fact, make a list using two columns.
In one column, list the pros of your man.
In the other column, list his cons.
You just might discover some thought-provoking facts.
You can't force a relationship to work
if the cons outweigh the pros.
If you force it, you will most likely regret it.
Listen to your spirit-mind and not your heart.
You can't make a round peg fit into a square hole.
Be wise!
Move on!

···

He heals the brokenhearted and binds their wounds.

Psalm 147:3

Part III

Friendship

A friend loves at all times.

Proverbs 17:17

A Faithful-Praying Friend
Is a Special Gift!

Of all your female relationships, one
of the greatest assets you
can have is the confidence that you have at least one friend
who not only prays, but prays for you.
If not daily, she prays for you often.
She's the kind of friend who prays
for you without asking her,
and the friend you can count on who always has your back.

Confess your sins to each other and pray for each other so
that you may be healed. The prayer of a righteous man is
powerful and effective.

James 5:16

You Have Two Friends That's for Sure!

My Beautiful Daughters,

Never forget you have two sure friends – God and me!

We will never give up on you!

The Father, Who is always there, never gave up on me,
will never give up on you – I am a witness!

I vow to never give up on you no matter what!

You have my unconditional love, a love you can pass on to
your sons and daughters, nephews,
nieces, and godchildren...

That's what moms do! That's who we are:

LOVE!

....

A friend loves at all times.

Proverbs 17:17

Girlfriends – Real Friends
Don't Cross Over the Line
Use Caution!

Never date a married man.
He belongs to somebody else.
That's stealing.

Never date your sister's or girlfriend's man.
You not only disrespect her, you disrespect yourself.

There are too many men from whom you
can either pick or choose.

It's all matter of character – integrity and respect.

Remember this:
"What goes around WILL come back around."

You WILL reap what you sow!

Be not deceived; God is not mocked; for whatsoever a man soweth, that shall he also reap.

Galatians 6:9

Women Can Be Friends, But Not All Necessarily Confidantes

Choose your female confidantes wisely.
Trust your first mind, some call it "your gut"
rather than trust your feelings and/or emotions.

Sincere and loyal friends cannot be measured
by all friends the same and not all can be trusted.

Beware of those who strive on self-
pity, have jealous natures,
and those others who define the phrase,
"Misery loves company."

Also, be cautious of those whom you know are envious.
The ones who never pay you a compliment
or applaud your accomplishments.

You know the kind… but keep on loving!
Friends are dimensional. That's what friendships are.

....

Faithful are the wounds of a friend: but the kisses of any enemy are deceitful.

Proverbs 27:6

Beware of Those So-called Friends

You'll discover some friends whom you thought
were friends are what one calls so-called friends.

Beware!

They will change on you!
You'll discover they aren't who you thought they were.

They will eventually show their true colors
by making negative comments
or criticize about how you look, what you
wear and even the decisions you make.
They rarely say anything positive
because they are so busy trying
to build up themselves by putting you and others down.

If you are not careful, they will treat
you the way you treat yourself.

If you respect yourself, they will respect you,
If you don't, it's your fault.

....

Faithful are the wounds of a friend; but the kisses of an enemy are deceitful.

Proverbs 27:6

More Thoughts to
Ponder About Friendship

Friends are our precious jewels and
should be valued as such.

Never take a friend for granted. Make it a
priority to let her know she's appreciated.

A true friend is not defined as being called
one, but because she always acts like one.

Don't be concerned about the number of friends you have.
You are richly blessed if you have just
one true friend who loves you.

Nothing compares to a faithful friend who believes in you
and prays for you because she knows the power of prayer.

You can call her 24/7 and she's there for you.
She makes you feel you are a priority.

Keep in mind, if you don't put high expectations
in friends, you'll be less disappointed.

Friends are dimensional. Some won't have staying
power. Others come into your life for a season.

Real friends don't hate on friends even in jest.

Friends always look for the best in you
and love you unconditionally.

---

*...there is a friend who sticks closer than a brother
[sister].*

Proverbs 18:24

Part IV

As The World Turns

As the World Turns Today…

Be so careful about the influences and trends of today.
Also, beware of some of the advice
given by notable experts.

Ensure their advice is in line with the Word of God.

It's vital to think for yourself, both
independently and critically,
but without judging.

Take pride in being your own person!

Be true to you!
Do You!

Beauty: The Real Deal…

Every woman desires to look and feel beautiful.
That's a good thing as long as you are
not trying to impress others
by following the culture and taking extreme measures like
having cosmetic surgery or a tummy tuck
to look perfect or be accepted.

What is so bad about maturing tenderly and gracefully?

Walk in your bold and beautiful self!

Think it!

Work it!

Don't allow the diet moguls, image
makers, or celebrities define
the real you based on their standards.
God created your body, soul, mind, and spirit
that are forever beautiful in His sight.

It's your inner beauty and self-confidence that define you.

Your body was made to change. It's your
choice to keep it under control.

Use common sense. It doesn't cost a dime.
You know the real deal: eat right; go to the
gym, work out, and get proper sleep.

Be committed to stay on track.
It's up to you!

True beauty stems from the inside out, not the outside in.
Set your own standards and validate you.

God reminds us "we are fearfully and wonderfully made."

---

*Charm is deceptive, and beauty is fleeting; but a woman
who fears the LORD is to be praised.*

Proverbs 31:10

There's the Good Stuff
and There's the Real Stuff

Take nothing for granted in our world today.
Be grateful for your accomplishments–
all you possess and prize.
They all come from God.
Never forget that He is your Provider
no matter what others believe or the world portrays.

Recognize the difference between good stuff and real stuff.

Keep your focus between the two.

The real stuff encompasses love of family and friends;
the things money can't buy.
That's the stuff that is real and lasts.

When you thank God for this-and-that
be very grateful for the real stuff.

The other comes and goes and often temporary.

Count your blessings–name them one by one.
You'll be amazed just how blessed you are.

But my God shall supply all you need according to His riches in glory by Jesus Christ.

Philippians 4:19

Success Can Be Fleeting, Stay Humble

Whether you have obtained wealth,
success, or fame, stay humble!

Successful or not, you are always
somebody in God's eyes as well as
those who love you – no matter what!

There's no success greater than God's
success when He has blessed you.
Man-given success can be temporal or fleeting.
God's success is what lasts.

Never forget to thank Him. He made it happen!
It might amaze you just how much
He will prosper you so you
can be a blessing to someone else.

It's been said, "Cleanliness is next to godliness." Humility is too!

....

For whoever exalts himself will be humbled, and whoever humbles himself will be exalted.

Matthew 23:12

The Key to Success:
Have a Plan and Work Your Plan

So you failed the exam the first time
and maybe even the second.

You applied to a college but didn't get accepted…

You applied for a few jobs but didn't get hired.

You feel discouraged and even like giving up.
Don't waste time beating yourself up.

Move on!

Don't take the easy way out! You can be your worst enemy.

General Colin Powell said it best:
*"There are no secrets to success. It is the result of preparation,
hard work, and learning from failure."*

In addition, self-discipline is just as important.

God never gives up on us, so don't give up on yourself!

Try! Try! and Try again!

For God did not give us a spirit of timidity, but a spirit of power of love and self-discipline.

II Timothy 1:7

Seek Wise Counsel, Always Consider Your Source

When you are going through tough
times and need to confide
in somebody you trust, connect with a friend/person,
who is not only trustworthy; but someone who is wise;
and knows God's Word and Jesus
Christ for herself/himself.

You can trust her/his input will be biblically
sound as well as morally based.

That person will care enough to help you make
the right decision or simply serve as a good listener
while keeping you in prayer.

The effectual fervent prayer of a righteous man availeth much.

James 5:16

Wise Decisions Should
Be Devoid of Emotions

Prayer should be your prerequisite
when making serious decisions.

Most hurts and heart-pain experiences are the result
of making decisions when emotional.
Sometimes, we become so emotional
that we leave God out
and the Enemy sneaks in and plays tricks with our minds.

Don't allow your emotions to rule your mind
or take you to a place you don't need to go
and perhaps you'll eventually regret.

Prayer is the answer!
Always stop to pray even if you don't feel like it.

...and call upon me in the day of trouble; I will deliver you and you will honor me.

Psalm 50:15

Love Is Action – Not Acting…
Let's Get Serious!

I LOVE YOU!

These are precious and serious words.
Don't say it if you don't mean it.

These three words are too powerful to play with…

Don't use or abuse them simply to
satisfy a selfish want or desire.

When you use or abuse words you don't
mean – eventually, you will lose!

Most likely, it will be someone you will come to regret.
If not in the present, but perhaps in the future.

Love does not delight in evil but rejoices with the truth. It always protects, always trusts, always hopes, and always perseveres.

I Corinthians 12:6-7

Part V

Marriage

God still holds
the institution sacred
First time, second time... especially for His
Believers

The LORD *God said,*
"It is not good for man to be alone.
I will make a helper suitable for him."

Genesis 2:18

Marriage is Work but Definitely Worth It!

(Isn't that true about anything worth having?)

Women often look at marriage through rose-colored glasses and can fool themselves, thinking that they and their mates have such a love for each other that they can solve any problem and their marriage will last forever. They soon discover, once the doors are closed, marriage is so much more…

A good marriage takes commitment and work!

Marriage is about the good times and bad times. Be prepared for the ouches, sensitive moments – even some tears; learning more about

having patience with each other; even hurting each other
unintentionally; and other issues you don't expect.

Even if you are equally/evenly-yoked there
will be problems and/or conflict.
However, it will be how you and your mate deal with
those two issues that will make the difference.

For example, it takes two to argue and deal with conflict.
Stay committed to resolving your problems together.
Try to remember to attack issues and never each other.

Consider talking about your concerns to seasoned,
married couples you respect and admire. They can give
you viable advice about the low valleys and the rewards.

No matter how crazy in love you are,
your precious love will be tested.

Your patience and understanding will go a
long way when there's disagreement.
Don't let emotions get in the way.
Respect and treat your mate like you
do your very best friend.

Finally, stay committed, not only to your mate, also investing in a healthy and happy marriage and making it work.

Above all, **keep Christ Jesus center** and you're bound to celebrate many anniversaries.

Love is patient, love is kind. It does not envy, it does not boast, it is not proud.

I Corinthians 13:4

In Times Like These, Good Men/Husbands Are Not Easy to Meet or Find

If you've been blessed to have found a
good husband, or he found you,
learn to treasure each other. Remember,
everyone has flaws and you do too.

It's important to keep the communication lines open.
Never shut down on him based on anger.
Express your feelings and listen to his too.
Never take him for granted. Treat him the
way you desire him to treat you.
If he makes you feel special, make him
feel special too. It goes both ways!

Think of ways to nurture and keep your relationship fresh.
If you had trust or other issues in past relationships,
don't allow the past to ruin your future. If you

never dealt with them, you should consider seeking
professional counseling with a licensed therapist.
Whatever you decide, keep God center.
Pray to him about your problems and seek His direction.

Plan a prayer-time together. Consider
it at least once a week.
Make Date Night a priority! Laugh a
lot and do fun things together.

Never go to bed without speaking because you
don't know what tomorrow will bring.
It very well could be the last time you see each other.

Here's a new one from me:
*"A couple who sticks and prays together
is destined to stay together."*

Be very mindful:

There are no perfect marriages, but there are great ones!
You CAN have that!

....

*Do not fear, for I am with you; do not be dismayed, for I
am your God. I will uphold you with my righteous right
hand.*

Isaiah 41:10

Work Together on Finding Solutions That Work for Two

Nobody is perfect yet we act like we want our mates to be, especially in a marriage.

It's so easy finding fault with one another.
It's the human condition.

It's also easy to complain about one thing or the other.

It takes stepping outside of oneself,
sensitivity, and humility to want
to find a solution to whatever the problem is.

Where there is a problem, there's always a solution!

Love is patient, love is kind…

I Corinthians 13:4

There's Nothing Like an Understanding

Understanding has more value than one can imagine.

It involves being a very good listener and communicator.

It makes a big difference to understand
the facts before jumping to
your own conclusions.

Whatever the problem or situation might
be consider the best solution
that will work for both.

Begin by being sensitive with an open mind;
also remember your mate is not a mind-reader.

You should not assume he knows what's bothering you,
simply because you think he does.

Learn to communicate your needs, desires, and concerns.
Keep in mind, early into the marriage that
you are still learning each other.
And you'll continue to learn and understand
each other over the years.

Understand?

....

...with all thy getting – get understanding.

Proverbs 4:7

Everyone Makes Mistakes
Allow Him to Make His

Don't be a nag.
Allow room for your man to make mistakes.

We all make mistakes because we're human.

Learn to agree to disagree and recognize the difference
between critiquing and criticizing.

Critiquing helps to build up when
it's done in the right spirit.

Criticizing and judging tear down. That's
the flesh and a critical spirit.

Have a Plan and Work Your Plan
Love should keep an open mind and not foster strife.

Love is always kind…

....

Let there be no strife between you and me.

Genesis 13:8

You Can't Fix Him
So Don't Try to Change Him

Purpose to try and see the good in your man.

Once you discover it, work on encouraging his good.

Affirm him and show you appreciate him as well.

Do not try to make him over according
to your specifications.

The positive results will not only surprise
you, they will bless the relationship.

Sometimes, for things to change for the
better – change begins with you.

Ask yourself, "Would I like it if he
tried to make me over?"

But let us encourage one another.

Hebrews 10:25

Personal Attacks Never Win

When trouble shows its ugly face, no matter who's at fault, it's important to repair the rift as soon as possible.

Try to come to a resolution where
you both are in agreement.

A reminder: Attack the problem and not each other.

What matters most is finding a way to fix it immediately.
Then you can return to what matters most
– love and peace among each other.

For thy love is better than wine.

Song of Solomon 1:2

Guard the Heart of Your Marriage

Think for a minute how you guard
your house; your car and
other prized possessions.

Be mindful to guard the heart of
your marriage much more.

Don't allow issues that have no value
to keep you from asking
for forgiveness when you know you are wrong.

Softening your heart, saying, "please
forgive me…" can open his heart.
Remember his heart is your heart—and your heart is his.

When two hearts are in harmony, you both must safeguard
tearing or breaking them apart.

Above all else, guard your heart, for it is the wellspring of life.

Proverbs 4:23

Affirm Your Man,
If Not Other Women Will

As wives, we should affirm our husbands.
We delight in being complimented,
pampered, and appreciated by them.

It's just as important that we do
special things for them too.
If you don't know what your man
needs from you, just ask him.

The Enemy is always lurking after
good honest married men,
especially who are low in spirit, feel
lonely, and unappreciated.

If we take our men for granted, there
are lots of women out there,

waiting in line, some who are desperate, and
others simply in search of a good man.
They will gladly give him affirmation if you don't.

Our relationships are in danger if we
leave our husbands out there.

We have the power to be victorious
as we keep trust in the Lord.

We do this by ensuring that our
husbands are our #1 priority.

---

*THE WISE woman builds her house, but with her own
hands, the foolish tears hers down.*

Proverbs 14:1

The Wise Woman Knows the Power of Prayer When It Comes to Her Marriage

A praying wife knows the power of
prayer and what an asset it is.

She not only prays during troubling times in
the marriage or about other concerns,
she never fails to pray for her husband.

She prays for his spiritual growth as well as her own.
She knows the significance in keeping
God center of the relationship,
especially in the world in which we live today.

She not only prays and thanks God for
the good times, she seeks Him
when she's going through bad times as well.

She believes in the power of prayer and God's faithfulness.

A wise woman/wife NEVER leaves God out!

For My thoughts are not your thoughts, nor are your ways My ways, declares the Lord.

Isaiah 55:8

Do the Right/Righteous Thing!

"Tit for Tat" never works.

Two wrongs never make a situation right.

Evil for evil fosters more evil.

It doesn't matter who hurts you or tries.

Always do the righteous thing!
It's not that difficult.

Pray for and learn to forgive your adversaries
– spouse, family, and friends alike.

The battle is never yours when you give it to the Lord.

Make sure that nobody pays wrong for wrong, but always try to be kind to each other and everyone else.

I Thessalonians 5:15

Forgiveness Though Difficult Should Keep No Record

Like a mother whose love keeps no record
of her son's or daughter's mistakes,
forgiveness in a marriage relationship deserves the same.

A mature love should be open to
forgiveness regarding your mate's
mistakes and wrongs that are unintentional.

Most mistakes will be minor – but not all.
Still, allow yourself to be open with a sense
of understanding and forgiveness.

Holding on and reminding him of his
mistakes each time you have a
disagreement will eventually take a toll on the relationship.

It's a matter of choice.

You can choose to forgive and move on or choose to be unhappy and miserable.

There are serious mistakes or violations that can break up a marriage or relationship. Regardless, God would have you to forgive.

It can be very difficult, but imprisoning yourself because you choose not to forgive is much worse.

Be kind and compassionate to one another, forgiving each other, just as in Christ God forgave you.

Ephesians 4:32

More Thoughts to Ponder About Forgiveness

FORGIVENESS: Just look to the cross and seriously think about what Jesus Christ did for you!

The act of forgiveness can be a difficult process. Sometimes, it takes forgiving your betrayer again and again. You should never stop trying. Why? Because God says so.

Forgiveness is a choice to either hold on or let go, although you won't forget. You have the power to let it go or make the situation more difficult for yourself.

If it's difficult to forgive and you are determined to hold a grudge, guess who will be held in bondage? Most likely, he will have moved on with his life.

When we ask God with a sincere heart for forgiveness, He not only forgives our sins and transgressions, He also tells us if we refuse to forgive our trespassers, He won't forgive us.

As far as the east is from the west, so far has He removed our transgressions from us.

Psalm 103:12

Part VI

Motherhood and Children

These commandments that I give you today
are to be upon your hearts.
Impress them on your children.
Talk about them when you sit at home
and when you walk along the road,
when you lie down and when you get up.

Deuteronomy 6:6-7

FAITH!
The Legacy That Lasts

Make it a commitment to pass on the
legacy of your faith to your children.

Aside from your love, affection, care, and
nurturing, there is no greater legacy
than for them to witness your faith in action.

Not only talk your faith, let them see you walk in it too.

Pray your faith, not only at their
bedside, let them see you pray
and live it before them daily.

You will be giving them a glimpse
who Jesus Christ is through
your consistent walk.
In return, prayerfully, they too will desire to follow Him.

It doesn't mean they won't have pitfalls; however, they will remember how you handled them.

Lo, children are an heritage of the Lord...

Psalm 127

Affirmation
and Spiritual Foundation
Go Hand and Hand

It's very important as a mom that you
not only give your children
love and affection, they too need affirmation and assurance
embraced by a strong spiritual foundation.

Teach them early on about the things of God.

Take them to church while they are
young, later enroll them
in Sunday/Church School.

Always remember, you are their example
of what faith in God means.
As their first witness, prayerfully, they
will pass on the experience

to the next generation.
Emphasize the value of being doers as
well as hearers of God's Word.
Don't just talk the talk, let them see you walk the walk.

Do not merely listen to the Word, and so deceive yourselves. Do what it says.

James 1:22

What You Believe in Matters—You Are Your Child's First Role Model and Teacher

Your children will learn a lot in school, but you and dad are their very first teachers.

Their instruction comes long before they are enrolled in school.

So, in all your teaching, teach by example.

Children are bright and intuitive, they will model what you do more than what you say.

They are always watching you!

Moms, it also pays to be mindful of the negative outside influences of today.

Train a child in the way he should go, and when he is old he will not depart from it.

Proverbs 22:6

Beware of Worldly Messages
and Identities
That Can Easily Sway Our Children

Mom and dad be positive role models for your children.
They can easily make some negative choices
from today's messages and trends.
Keep communication channels open and
lead them in the right direction.
It might not be easy, but if you don't, just
look at their choices that will:
television, movies, music; super-heroes,
celebrities, and the negativity
on their computers, etc.,
They will adopt their lifestyles dress
codes, habits, and speech, etc.
if you fail to set standards for them.
It's a reality, they still might stray, but
you can take comfort having

taught them in the way they should
go, and most importantly,
put and leave them in the hands of God.

There is no blueprint, but there's a Book
that has answers if you go there:
The Holy Scriptures – God's Inspired Word.

---

*Train a child in the way he should go and when he is old
he will not turn from it.*

Proverbs 22:6

More Thoughts to Ponder about Children

Children need to see role models within the family beginning with their parents as well as grandparents, aunts, uncles, and extended family.

Most parents desire to give their children the best childhood they can, and in some cases, they can't afford. The question is what is "best"? And what is it they'll remember and value most when they become adults and most likely parents? Be committed to give them wonderful childhood memories they can share when they become parents. It's what you input in them as little ones that they'll output as big ones... Love and hug them a lot–just because...

Family values are still what works and benefits children.

Children will follow your example
more than your advice.

Speak words of love and encouragement–
words that uplift not tear them down, so they
will communicate them to their children.

Set a time for morning prayer
before they leave for school.

Take them to children's church, but
first, teach them how to act.

Praise them for their good behavior,
accomplishments, and other deeds.

Admonish or punish them for poor
behavior; don't promise … do it! And <u>always</u>
encourage them to do what's right.
Teach them to give and not expect
something in return.

Teach them to show their appreciation when
someone does something nice for them by calling
(not texting) or sending a thank-you card.

TEACH THEM:

to exercise self-discipline, self-respect, and
to respect others as well as their elders.

good manners and to always be polite
to others: to say "yes and no,"
"thank-you," "please," "excuse me" and "I'm sorry!"

to always treat others the way they want to be treated and
that winners always tell the truth but losers lie.

bullying is for the weak and it's definitely a no-no!
Emphasize there **will be** consequences.

THE END

ALL PRAISE TO OUR LIVING GOD!

I TRULY LOVE THE LORD...

I learned my first Bible verse when I was a little girl around five years old. It was John 3:16: *For God so loved the world that He gave His only begotten Son, that whosoever believeth in Him should not perish, but have ever lasting life.* Although I was too young to fully comprehend that verse I never forgot it! Six years later, my mother died. I was eleven years old. I missed and grieved for her into my early thirties, but never questioned God why He took her from my three siblings and me. Although I suffered for a long time, I continued to trust God and believed that He never makes mistakes. As I matured and truly comprehended the meaning of John 3:16, it gave me peace and confidence that I would see my mother in Paradise. This I know:

> *There is only One answer to all our problems,*
> *all our sorrows and all our prayers.*

Only GOD!

L. K. ALEXANDER-BEDFORD is a native of Philadelphia, Pennsylvania. Her career as a newspaper journalist and public relations practitioner spanned over forty plus years covering three states – Pennsylvania, California, and Delaware. She retired in 1996 as Information Officer and Editor of *The Communicator*, house organ of the Peninsula-Delaware Conference of the United Methodist Church. A trailblazer in her own right, Alexander-Bedford was the first person of color hired as newspaper editor in one of the sixty-seven Annual Conferences in the UMC during that time. She is enjoying her retirement in Atlanta, Georgia, with her husband Joseph and two daughters, Lisa and Alexis, who live nearby. Above all, she appreciates her peace, contentment, and having more time to commune with God and serving others. Her platform has been encouraging young women, far and near, especially those who do not have close or positive relationships with their mothers.